Romance at Bluebird Inn

Lisa Head

Romance at Bluebird Inn

Copyright © 2023 Lisa Head

All right s reserved.

ISBN: 9798391594574

DEDICATION

I want to thank all my friends and family. Thank you all for the support and love you show to me and others. I especially want to thank my sons, Aiden, Randall and Jesse, for being my rock and comic relief. My love all of you!

Romance at Bluebird Inn

CONTENTS

Romance at Bluebird Inn

Romance at Bluebird Inn

Romance at Bluebird Inn

CHAPTER 1

As the sun began to set over the rolling hills, Sarah took a deep breath and stepped out of her car. She had arrived at the bed and breakfast where she would be spending the next few weeks, working on her latest book. As an author, she often sought out quiet and peaceful places to write, and this charming little inn seemed to fit the bill perfectly.

As she made her way to the front door, a tall, ruggedly handsome man emerged from the building. He wore a worn leather jacket and jeans that hugged his muscular thighs. His hair was tousled, as if he had just run his fingers through it, and his deep blue eyes twinkled in the fading light.

"Welcome to the Bluebird Inn," he said, his voice low and husky. "I'm Jack, the owner."

Sarah couldn't help but feel a flutter in her stomach at the sight of him. She had always been drawn to men who were a little rough around the edges, and Jack definitely fit the bill.

"Hi, I'm Sarah," she said, extending her hand.

Jack took her hand in his and gave it a firm shake. "It's nice to meet you, Sarah. Let me show you to your room."

As they walked through the cozy inn, Sarah couldn't help but notice the way Jack's eyes lingered on her. She felt a blush creeping up her cheeks, and she quickly looked away.

When they reached her room, Jack opened the door and gestured for her to enter. The room was small but cozy, with a queen-sized bed and a desk positioned by the window.

"I hope this will be to your liking," Jack said, his eyes never leaving her face.

"It's perfect," Sarah said, smiling up at him.

As Jack turned to leave, Sarah suddenly found herself overcome with an urge to reach out and touch him. Before she could stop herself, she reached out and laid a hand on his arm.

"Thank you," she said, her voice barely above a whisper.

Jack turned back to her, his eyes searching hers. Without another word, he leaned down and pressed his lips to hers. The kiss was gentle at first, but quickly deepened into something more passionate.

As they pulled away, Sarah couldn't believe what had just happened. She had only just met Jack, but already she felt a connection to him that she couldn't explain.

"Goodnight, Sarah," Jack said, his voice rough with desire.

"Goodnight, Jack," Sarah replied, already looking forward to tomorrow.

Sarah lay in bed, her heart racing and her mind reeling. She couldn't believe what had just happened between her and Jack. It had been so unexpected, yet so incredibly thrilling.

As she lay there, staring up at the ceiling, she wondered what Jack was thinking. Was he regretting the kiss already? Or did he feel the same spark of attraction that she did?

With a sigh, Sarah forced herself to push those thoughts aside. She was here to work, not to get involved with the owner of the inn. Besides, she had always been wary of relationships. Her last one had ended in heartbreak, and she didn't want to go through that again.

The next morning, Sarah woke up early and headed to the inn's dining room for breakfast. Jack was already there, sitting at a table in the corner with a cup of coffee.

"Good morning," he said, standing up as she approached. "Did you sleep well?"

"I did, thanks," Sarah replied, trying to act as if the kiss had never happened.

As they chatted over breakfast, Sarah found herself relaxing in Jack's company. He was easy to talk to and had a sense of humor that made her laugh. Before she knew it, they had been sitting there for an hour, lost in conversation.

As Sarah got up to leave, Jack stood up as well. "Do you have any plans for the day?" he asked.

Sarah shook her head. "No, I was just planning on working on my book."

"Would you like some company?" Jack asked, a hint of a smile playing at the corners of his mouth.

Sarah hesitated for a moment before nodding. "Sure, that sounds nice."

And with that, they spent the day together, exploring the town and getting to know each other better. By the time they returned to the inn that evening, Sarah knew that she was in trouble. She was falling for Jack, and there was no turning back.

As the day drew to a close, Sarah found herself lost in thought. She and Jack had spent the entire day together, laughing, talking, and enjoying each other's company. She couldn't believe how easy it was to be around him, how natural it felt to be in his presence.

As they walked back to the inn, Sarah couldn't resist stealing glances at Jack. She couldn't deny the attraction she felt for him, but at the same time, she knew that getting involved with him would be risky. She had come here to focus on her writing, not to fall in love.

But as they reached the door to her room, Jack turned to face her. "Sarah," he said, his voice soft. "I know we've only just met, but I can't stop thinking about you. Will you give me a chance? Will you go out with me tonight?"

Sarah's heart skipped a beat at his words. She wanted to say yes, wanted to throw caution to the wind and see where things could go with Jack. But at the same time, she knew that she couldn't let herself get distracted from her work.

"I don't know," she said, her voice barely above a whisper. "I'm here to work on my book, and I don't want to get sidetracked."

"I understand," Jack said, his face falling. "But if you change your mind, you know where to find me."

With that, he turned and walked away, leaving Sarah standing there feeling conflicted and confused. She knew that she wanted to be with him, but at the same time, she knew that she couldn't afford to get distracted.

As she lay in bed that night, Sarah knew that she had a decision to make. Would she give in to her feelings and take a chance on Jack? Or would she stay focused on her work and leave things between them as they were? Only time would tell, but for now, she was content to let her thoughts wander as she drifted off to sleep.

CHAPTER 2

The next morning, Sarah woke up feeling more rested than she had in a long time. As she got dressed and headed to the dining room for breakfast, she couldn't help but think about Jack and the way he had made her feel the day before.

When she arrived, she found Jack already sitting at a table with a cup of coffee. He looked up and smiled when he saw her.

"Good morning," he said, standing up to greet her. "How did you sleep?"

"Very well, thanks," Sarah replied, returning his smile. "How about you?"

"I slept like a baby," Jack said, grinning. "I'm glad to hear you did too."

As they sat down to eat breakfast together, Sarah found herself once again drawn into easy conversation with Jack. They talked about everything and nothing, and Sarah felt herself relaxing in his company.

After breakfast, Sarah headed back to her room to get some work done on her book. She had a deadline coming up, and she knew she couldn't afford to waste any time.

But as she sat down at her desk and began to type, her mind kept wandering back to Jack. She couldn't help but think about the way he had looked at her, the way he had made her laugh, the way he had made her feel.

Before she knew it, hours had passed, and Sarah had barely written a word. She was hopelessly distracted by thoughts of Jack and the way he had made her feel.

As the day wore on, Sarah knew that she had to make a decision. She couldn't keep letting herself get distracted like this. She had to choose between her work and her feelings for Jack.

That evening, as she sat in her room, Sarah made up her mind. She couldn't resist the pull she felt toward Jack any longer. She had to see where things could go between them.

With a deep breath, Sarah made her way to the inn's dining room, where Jack was waiting for her.

"Hey," he said, his face lighting up as he saw her. "How was your day?"

"It was fine," Sarah said, smiling nervously. "But there's something I need to talk to you about."

"Sure," Jack said, looking at her curiously. "What is it?"

"I know I said that I didn't want to get sidetracked from my work," Sarah began, her voice shaking slightly. "But the truth is, I can't stop thinking about you. I don't want to let this opportunity slip away. I want to give us a chance."

As she spoke, Sarah could feel her heart racing. She didn't know what Jack would say, but she knew that she had to be honest with him.

To her relief, Jack's face broke into a huge smile. "I was hoping you'd say that" he said, taking her hand in his. "I feel the same way about you, Sarah. I want to see where this goes."

With that, Sarah and Jack spent the rest of the evening talking and laughing, lost in their newfound connection. As the night wore on, Sarah knew that she had made the right decision. She couldn't wait to see what the future held for her and Jack.

The days that followed were a blur of writing and spending time with Jack. Sarah found that she was able to balance her work and her newfound romance with Jack, and it was like nothing she had ever experienced before.

They explored the town together, taking long walks and discovering hidden gems along the way. They spent evenings sitting in front of the fire, talking and laughing until the early hours of the morning.

As Sarah got to know Jack better, she realized that he was everything she had been looking for. He was kind, intelligent, and funny, and he made her feel alive in a way she hadn't felt in years.

But as much as Sarah was enjoying her time with Jack, she couldn't help but feel a twinge of guilt. She had come to this town to focus on her writing, and she was worried that she was losing sight of that goal.

One afternoon, as they sat together in a quiet park, Sarah voiced her concerns to Jack.

"I feel like I'm not getting enough work done," she said, her voice tinged with worry. "I'm falling behind on my deadlines, and I don't want to let my agent down."

Jack looked at her with understanding in his eyes. "I get it," he said. "But Sarah, you're doing great.

You've written more in the past few days than you have in weeks. Don't be so hard on yourself."

Sarah nodded, grateful for Jack's words of encouragement. As they sat in the park together, she felt a sense of peace wash over her. With Jack by her side, she knew that she could do anything.

As the sun began to set, Sarah and Jack made their way back to the inn. As they walked hand in hand, Sarah couldn't help but feel grateful for the way things had turned out.

She had come to this town with a specific goal in mind, but she had found something even more precious along the way. With Jack by her side, Sarah knew that anything was possible.

That night, as they sat together by the fire, Sarah couldn't help but think about how much her life had changed in just a few short days. She had come to this town with a heavy heart, burdened by the weight of her responsibilities and her own expectations.

But now, with Jack by her side, she felt lighter, freer. She could feel herself letting go of her worries, her fears, and her doubts, and it was all thanks to him.

As they talked and laughed together, Sarah realized that she was falling deeper and deeper in love with Jack. She didn't know what the future held for them, but she knew that she didn't want to let him go.

Before she knew it, the night had grown late, and Sarah knew it was time to say goodnight. As she got up to leave, Jack stood up as well.

"I had a great time tonight," he said, taking her hand in his. "I'm so glad we found each other."

"Me too," Sarah said, smiling up at him. "I don't think I've ever felt this way before."

"Neither have I," Jack said, leaning in to kiss her. As their lips met, Sarah felt a rush of warmth spread through her body. She knew in that moment that she had found something truly special.

As Sarah made her way back to her room, she couldn't stop smiling. She felt like she was on top of the world, and nothing could bring her down. With Jack by her side, she knew that she could conquer anything.

As she drifted off to sleep that night, Sarah felt grateful for the unexpected twist her life had taken. She didn't know what the future held, but she knew that as long as she had Jack by her side, she could handle anything that came her way.

CHAPTER 3

The next few days passed in a blur of writing and spending time with Jack. Sarah found herself falling more and more in love with him with each passing moment. She had never felt so connected to anyone before, and she knew that she never wanted to let him go.

Despite her initial worries about falling behind on her writing, Sarah found that she was making great progress on her novel. With Jack's support and encouragement, she felt more inspired than ever before.

One afternoon, as they sat together in a coffee shop, Sarah found herself lost in thought. She had been thinking about the future and what it might hold for her and Jack.

"Jack," she said, breaking the comfortable silence between them. "Do you ever think about the future?"

Jack looked at her, his brow furrowing slightly. "What do you mean?" he asked.

"I mean, do you ever think about what's going to happen after this?" Sarah said, gesturing to the town around them. "After we go back to our normal lives?"

Jack nodded thoughtfully. "Of course, I do," he said. "But I try not to worry too much about it. Right now, I'm just enjoying being here with you."

Sarah nodded, feeling a sense of relief wash over her. She had been worried that she was the only one thinking about the future.

But as much as she tried to push her worries aside, they lingered in the back of her mind. She couldn't help but wonder what would happen when they went back to their normal lives.

As the days passed, Sarah found herself becoming more and more anxious. She knew that she had to talk to Jack about her concerns, but she didn't want to ruin the perfect bubble they had created for themselves.

One evening, as they sat together in front of the fire, Sarah took a deep breath and spoke up.

"Jack, I need to talk to you about something," she said, her voice trembling slightly.

Jack looked at her with concern in his eyes. "What's wrong?" he asked.

Sarah took another deep breath before speaking. "I'm just worried about what's going to happen when we go back to our normal lives," she said. "I don't want to lose you."

Jack reached out and took her hand, squeezing it gently. "Sarah, I don't want to lose you either," he said. "But we can't let our worries about the future ruin the present. Let's just enjoy the time we have together."

Sarah nodded, feeling a sense of relief wash over her. She knew that Jack was right. They couldn't control the future, but they could make the most of the present.

As they sat together in front of the fire, Sarah felt grateful for the love and support of the man sitting next to her. With Jack by her side, she knew that anything was possible.

The next morning, Sarah woke up feeling refreshed and rejuvenated. She had spent the night wrapped in Jack's arms, and for the first time in days, she had slept soundly.

As she made her way to the coffee shop, Sarah felt

a sense of excitement in the pit of her stomach. She couldn't wait to spend the day with Jack, writing and exploring the town.

But as she walked into the coffee shop, she saw something that made her heart sink. Sitting at a table in the corner was a woman, laughing and chatting with Jack.

Sarah's mind raced as she tried to keep her emotions in check. Who was this woman? And why was Jack sitting with her?

As she made her way over to their table, Sarah tried to push her fears and doubts aside. Maybe it was just an old friend, she told herself. Maybe she was overreacting.

"Hey Sarah," Jack said, smiling up at her as she approached the table. "This is my friend Rachel. Rachel, this is Sarah."

Sarah forced a smile as she shook Rachel's hand. She couldn't help but feel a twinge of jealousy as she watched the two of them talking and laughing together.

As the day went on, Sarah tried to ignore her feelings of jealousy and focus on her writing. But no matter how hard she tried, she couldn't shake the image of Jack and Rachel from her mind.

That night, as they sat together in front of the fire, Sarah found herself struggling to keep her emotions in check.

"Jack," she said, her voice trembling slightly. "Can we talk?"

"Of course," Jack said, turning to face her. "What's on your mind?"

Sarah took a deep breath before speaking. "I saw you with Rachel today," she said. "And I couldn't help but feel jealous."

Jack's expression softened as he reached out to take her hand. "Sarah, Rachel is just a friend," he said. "I care about you. You're the one I want to be with."

Sarah nodded, feeling a sense of relief wash over her. She knew that Jack was telling the truth.

As they sat together in front of the fire, Sarah felt grateful for Jack's reassurance. She knew that their love was real, and that nothing could come between them. Together, they would face whatever the future held.

The next day, Sarah and Jack spent the morning

exploring the town. They visited quaint bookshops and cafes, and Sarah took notes for her book as they wandered through the streets.

As they sat down for lunch, Sarah felt a sense of contentment settle over her. She was happy to be with Jack, and she knew that he felt the same way.

But as they ate, Sarah couldn't help but feel a sense of unease. She knew that there was still so much she didn't know about Jack, and she worried that their pasts might come back to haunt them.

"Jack," she said, setting down her sandwich. "There's something I need to tell you."

"What is it?" Jack asked, looking up at her.

Sarah took a deep breath. "I haven't been completely honest with you," she said. "There are things in my past that I haven't told you about."

Jack's expression didn't change, but Sarah could feel the tension in the air. "What kind of things?" he asked.

Sarah hesitated before speaking. "I was in an abusive relationship," she said. "It's something I've never talked about with anyone before."

Jack reached out to take her hand. "Sarah, I'm so

sorry," he said. "You don't have to tell me anything you don't want to. But if you ever need to talk, I'm here for you."

Sarah felt a sense of relief wash over her. She knew that she had made the right choice in telling Jack about her past.

As they finished their lunch, Sarah felt a sense of hopefulness for their future together. She knew that they still had a lot to learn about each other, but she was willing to take the risk.

Together, they would face whatever the future held, and Sarah was excited to see where their love would take them.

CHAPTER 4

The next few days were filled with writing and exploring for Sarah and Jack. They visited local landmarks and wrote for hours, their laptops side by side.

But as they worked, Sarah couldn't shake the feeling that something was off. She had noticed that Jack had been receiving more calls and texts than usual, and she couldn't help but wonder who was on the other end of those messages.

One afternoon, as they sat in a small park, Sarah decided to confront Jack about her concerns.

"Jack," she said, looking up from her notebook. "I've noticed that you've been getting a lot of calls and texts lately. Is everything okay?"

Jack's expression turned serious. "Yeah, it's just work stuff," he said. "Nothing for you to worry about."

But Sarah wasn't convinced. She had a feeling that Jack was hiding something from her.

"Jack, I don't want to push, but I just want to make sure that we're being completely honest with each other," she said. "Is there something you're not telling me?"

Jack hesitated before speaking. "Sarah, there is something," he said. "It's just...complicated."

Sarah's heart sank as Jack began to speak. He told her about an ex-girlfriend who had recently come back into his life, and how he had been struggling with his feelings for her.

"I'm sorry, Sarah," Jack said, his voice filled with regret. "I never wanted to hurt you. I just didn't know how to handle the situation."

Sarah felt a sense of betrayal wash over her. She had thought that she and Jack had something special, but now she wasn't so sure.

As they walked back to their cabin, Sarah couldn't help but feel a sense of despair. She had opened up to Jack about her past, but now it seemed that he was keeping secrets from her.

That night, as they lay in bed, Sarah couldn't sleep. She tossed and turned, her mind racing with thoughts of Jack and his ex-girlfriend.

Finally, unable to take it anymore, she turned to face him.

"Jack," she said, her voice trembling. "I need to know something. Do you still have feelings for her?"

Jack hesitated before speaking. "I don't know," he said. "But what I do know is that I care about you, Sarah. You're the one I want to be with."

Sarah nodded, feeling a sense of relief wash over her. She knew that she loved Jack, but she also knew that she couldn't compete with his past.

As they lay in bed, Sarah made a decision. She would give Jack the benefit of the doubt, but she would also be careful. She wouldn't let herself get hurt again.

Together, they would face whatever challenges came their way, but Sarah knew that their love would be put to the test.

The next day, Sarah and Jack decided to take a break from writing and explore the nearby hiking trails. As they walked, Sarah couldn't help but feel a sense of distance between them. She had hoped that their conversation the previous night would have brought them closer together, but she couldn't shake the feeling that Jack was still holding something back.

"Sarah, can we talk for a minute?" Jack said, breaking the silence.

"Of course," she replied, looking up at him.

Jack took a deep breath. "I know that I messed up," he said. "But I want you to know that I care about you, and I'm willing to do whatever it takes to make things right."

Sarah felt a sense of hopefulness wash over her. She knew that Jack was sincere, but she still had doubts.

"Jack, I want to believe you," she said. "But I need to know that you're being honest with me."

Jack nodded. "I understand," he said. "And I promise that I will be completely honest with you from now on."

Sarah smiled, feeling a sense of relief wash over her. She knew that it wouldn't be easy, but she was willing to give Jack another chance.

As they continued on the trail, Sarah couldn't help but feel grateful for the natural beauty around them. The leaves rustled in the breeze, and the sun shone down on their faces.

In that moment, Sarah knew that she had made the

right decision in giving Jack another chance. She didn't know what the future held, but she was willing to take the risk.

Together, they would face whatever challenges came their way, and Sarah was excited to see where their love would take them.

As they reached the end of the trail, Jack took Sarah's hand and pulled her close.

"Sarah, I want you to know that I love you," he said, looking into her eyes.

Sarah's heart swelled with emotion. She knew that Jack was being sincere, and she felt the same way.

"I love you too, Jack," she said, leaning in for a kiss.

As they embraced, Sarah knew that their love was stronger than any obstacle that they might face. She had faith in their future, and she was ready to face whatever challenges came their way.

Together, they walked back to their cabin, hand in hand, ready to start a new chapter in their love story.

CHAPTER 5

Sarah and Jack spent the rest of their time at the cabin enjoying each other's company. They explored the nearby town, tried new restaurants, and spent lazy afternoons reading by the lake.

As the end of their trip approached, Sarah couldn't help but feel a sense of sadness. She didn't want to leave the peacefulness of the cabin and the newfound closeness with Jack.

On their last night, Jack surprised her with a candlelit dinner on the porch of their cabin. As they ate, he reached into his pocket and pulled out a small box.

"Sara, I know that we've only known each other for a short time," he said, opening the box to reveal a delicate silver ring. "But I feel a deep connection with you, and I want to take the next step. Sarah, will you be my girlfriend?"

Tears welled up in Sarah's eyes as she nodded her head. "Yes, Jack. I want to be with you," she said.

As Jack slipped the ring onto her finger, Sarah felt a sense of joy that she had never experienced before. She knew that there would be challenges ahead, but she was ready to face them with Jack by her side.

The rest of the night was filled with laughter, music, and conversation. They danced on the porch, and under the stars, they shared their hopes and dreams for the future.

As they packed up their belongings the next day and prepared to leave the cabin, Sarah couldn't help but feel a sense of hope for the future. She knew that their love was still new and untested, but she had faith that it would only grow stronger with time.

As they drove away, Sarah looked out the window at the beautiful landscape and felt a sense of gratitude for the experiences she had shared with Jack. She knew that they had a long journey ahead, but with love as their guide, she was ready to take on whatever the future held.

As they made their way back to the city, Sarah and Jack talked excitedly about their plans for the future. They discussed moving in together and starting a life together. Sarah couldn't believe how much her life had changed in just a few short weeks.

When they arrived back in the city, Jack took Sarah to a fancy restaurant to celebrate their newfound relationship. Over dinner, they talked about their favorite memories from their trip and shared stories from their past.

As the night wore on, Sarah couldn't help but feel grateful for the way things had turned out. She had never expected to find love so quickly, but she knew that Jack was the one for her.

As they left the restaurant and walked hand in hand down the city streets, Sarah felt a sense of contentment that she had never experienced before. She knew that there would be challenges ahead, but she was confident that they could face them together.

Back at Jack's apartment, they cuddled on the couch and watched a movie. Sarah leaned her head on Jack's shoulder, feeling safe and secure in his arms. As the credits rolled, Jack turned to her and took her face in his hands.

"Sarah, I know that we've only been together for a short time," he said. "But I want you to know that I love you. I've never felt this way about anyone before, and I want to spend the rest of my life with you."

Tears welled up in Sarah's eyes as she looked into Jack's loving gaze. "I love you too, Jack," she said, knowing that she had found her soulmate.

As they embraced, Sarah knew that they had a bright future ahead of them. They had found love in the most unexpected of places, and she knew that it was meant to

For the rest of the night, they talked about their hopes and dreams for the future. Sarah knew that their relationship was still new, but she felt confident that they could build a strong foundation for their love.

As the night turned into morning, Sarah and Jack fell asleep in each other's arms, feeling content and happy. Sarah knew that her life had changed for the better since meeting Jack, and she couldn't wait to see what the future held for them.

Over the next few weeks, Sarah and Jack spent every moment they could together. They explored the city, went on romantic dates, and shared intimate moments. Sarah felt like she was on cloud nine, and she knew that Jack felt the same way.

As their relationship deepened, Sarah and Jack knew that it was time to take the next step. Jack took Sarah to the beach at sunset and got down on one knee. He pulled out a ring and asked her to be his wife.

Tears streamed down Sarah's face as she said yes. She couldn't believe how much her life had changed in such a short time, and she knew that she was ready to spend the rest of her life with Jack.

As they hugged each other tightly, Sarah knew that their love was strong enough to overcome any obstacle. She felt grateful for every moment they had shared together, and she knew that their future was bright.

With a newfound sense of hope and happiness, Sarah and Jack looked forward to starting the next chapter of their lives together.

CHAPTER 6

Sarah and Jack spent the next few months planning their wedding. They decided to have a small ceremony with just their closest family and friends.

Sarah couldn't believe how much work went into planning a wedding. There were so many details to attend to, from choosing the flowers to deciding on the menu. But with Jack by her side, she knew that they could handle anything that came their way.

As the wedding day approached, Sarah grew more and more excited. She couldn't wait to start her life with Jack as his wife.

On the day of the wedding, Sarah woke up early and spent the morning getting ready with her bridesmaids. She put on her beautiful white dress and took a deep breath, feeling a sense of calm wash over her.

As she walked down the aisle, she saw Jack waiting for her at the end. He looked handsome in his suit, and Sarah couldn't help but smile as she approached him.

The ceremony was beautiful and heartfelt, and Sarah and Jack exchanged their vows in front of their loved ones. As they kissed for the first time as husband and wife, Sarah knew that this was the beginning of a new chapter in their lives together.

The reception was filled with laughter and love, as everyone celebrated the happy couple. Sarah and Jack danced together under the stars, feeling like they were the only ones in the world.

As the night drew to a close, Sarah and Jack said goodbye to their guests and headed off on their honeymoon. They spent two weeks in a romantic paradise, exploring the beaches and enjoying each other's company.

When they returned home, Sarah and Jack settled into their new life together as husband and wife. They faced challenges along the way, but they always worked through them with love and support.

Years later, Sarah looked back on that first fateful meeting with Jack and smiled. She knew that it was destiny that brought them together, and she was grateful every day for the love they shared. No

After their honeymoon, Sarah and Jack returned home to start their lives together as a married couple. They moved into a cozy little house on the outskirts of town and began to build a life together.

Sarah found a job as a teacher at a local school, and Jack continued to work as a software engineer. They were both busy with their jobs, but they always made time for each other.

On the weekends, they explored the city, tried new restaurants, and went on road trips. They also made time for quiet nights at home, where they would cook dinner together and watch their favorite movies.

As the years passed, Sarah and Jack grew even closer. They faced new challenges together, including the loss of Sarah's father and the birth of their two children. But through it all, they remained devoted to each other.

Sarah often thought back to their wedding day and how happy she felt. She knew that their love had only grown stronger since then, and she was grateful for every moment they shared.

On their tenth wedding anniversary, Sarah and Jack renewed their vows in a beautiful ceremony surrounded by their family and friends. It was a celebration of their love and commitment to each other, and Sarah felt grateful for every moment they had spent together.

As the night drew to a close, Sarah looked around at the people she loved and knew that her life was complete. She had found her soulmate in Jack, and she knew that they would be together forever.

With a heart full of love and gratitude, Sarah hugged her husband tightly and whispered, "I love you." And in that moment, she knew that they were exactly where they were meant to be.

Years turned into decades, and Sarah and Jack grew old together. They had weathered many storms over the years, but their love had only grown stronger with each passing day.

As they sat together on their front porch, watching the sunset, Sarah reflected on the life they had built together. She felt a deep sense of gratitude for all the love and happiness that they had shared.

Jack took her hand and smiled at her; his eyes filled with love. "I'm so glad I met you all those years ago," he said. "I can't imagine my life without you."

Sarah squeezed his hand back and smiled. "Me neither," she said. "You're my soulmate, Jack. And I love you more than anything in this world."

They sat there in comfortable silence, enjoying each other's company as the sun slowly disappeared below the horizon. And in that moment, they knew that they had everything they could ever need, as long as they had each other.

As the night grew dark, Sarah and Jack went inside, holding hands and feeling grateful for the life they had built together. They knew that they would face more challenges in the years to come, but they also knew that they had the strength and love to face them together.

And with that thought in their hearts, they settled into bed, feeling content and at peace. For they knew that they were exactly where they were meant to be, in each other's.

CHAPTER 7

Sarah woke up to the sound of birds chirping outside her window. She stretched and yawned, feeling well-rested and content. As she got out of bed, she looked over at Jack, who was still sleeping peacefully. She smiled to herself, feeling grateful for her loving husband.

As she got dressed and headed downstairs, she heard a knock at the door. She wondered who could be visiting so early in the morning but went to answer it anyway.

To her surprise, it was her old friend, Emily, whom she hadn't seen in years. They hugged each other tightly, catching up on old times and reminiscing about their wild college days.

After a while, Emily looked at Sarah seriously. "I'm actually here because I need your help," she said. "I'm going through a really tough time right now, and I don't know who else to turn to."

Sarah listened attentively as Emily told her about her recent breakup and the challenges she was facing in her job. She could see the pain and sadness in Emily's eyes and knew that she needed a friend.

Without hesitation, Sarah invited Emily inside and made her a cup of coffee. She listened as Emily poured out her heart, offering comfort and support.

As they sat together, Sarah realized how much she had grown over the years. She was no longer the same carefree college student who had partied all night and skipped classes. She was now a mature woman who had a stable job, a loving husband, and a family to take care of.

But she also realized that she still had the same heart, full of love and compassion. And she knew that she could use that love to help others, just as she was doing now for her dear friend.

As Emily left later that day, Sarah felt a sense of satisfaction and fulfillment. She had been able to help someone in need, and it made her feel good.

She went back to Jack, feeling grateful for his love and support. And as they sat together, talking about the day ahead, Sarah realized that life was full of unexpected surprises, but as long as she had

Jack by her side, she knew that she could face anything.

As the day went on, Sarah couldn't shake the feeling that she needed to do more for Emily. She knew that her friend was going through a tough time, and she wanted to help her in any way she could.

After some thought, Sarah decided to invite Emily over for dinner that night. She wanted to create a warm and welcoming space for her friend, a place where she could forget about her troubles for a while and just enjoy good company.

As she prepared dinner, Sarah felt a sense of excitement and anticipation. She had always loved cooking, and she was looking forward to sharing her passion with Emily.

When Emily arrived, Sarah greeted her with a warm hug and a smile. She showed her friend around the house, sharing stories about the different rooms and decorations.

As they sat down to dinner, Sarah watched as Emily's face lit up with joy. The food was delicious, and the conversation flowed easily. They talked about everything from old memories to new dreams, and Sarah could feel the connection between them growing stronger.

After dinner, they sat outside on the porch, watching the stars twinkle in the night sky. Emily turned to his Sarah, her eyes full of gratitude. "Thank you for tonight," she said. "I needed this more than you know."

Sarah smiled back at her. "Anytime, my dear friend," she said. "That's what friends are for."

As they said their goodbyes and Emily headed home, Sarah felt a sense of happiness and contentment. She knew that life was full of challenges, but she also knew that love and friendship could help her overcome anything.

As she settled into bed next to Jack, she couldn't help but feel grateful for the life she had built. She had a loving husband, a beautiful home, and wonderful friends. And she knew that no matter what the future held, she was ready to face it with an open heart and a strong spirit.

As Sarah drifted off to sleep, she thought about the conversation she had with Emily. She realized that sometimes, all people needed was a listening ear and a shoulder to lean on. And she felt grateful that she was able to provide that for her friend.

The next morning, Sarah woke up feeling refreshed and ready to start the day. She and Jack had plans to go for a hike in the nearby mountains, and she was looking forward to spending some quality time with her husband in the great outdoors.

As they reached the summit, Sarah looked out at the breathtaking view of the valley below. She felt a sense of peace and tranquility wash over her. She was reminded of the beauty and wonder of the world, and she felt grateful to be alive and surrounded by love.

As they made their way back down the trail, Sarah couldn't help but feel grateful for all the blessings in her life. She had a wonderful husband, a supportive family, and great friends. And she knew that no matter what challenges lay ahead, she would always have the love and support she needed to get through them.

As they returned home, Sarah felt a sense of contentment and satisfaction. She was reminded that life was a journey, full of ups and downs, but as long as she had love in her heart, she knew that she could overcome anything.

She curled up on the couch next to Jack, feeling the warmth of his embrace. As they watched the sunset together, Sarah knew that life was good, and she felt grateful for every moment of it.

CHAPTER 8

The weeks flew by, and Sarah was caught up in the whirlwind of work and family life. She was constantly busy with her job and taking care of her home, but she always made time for her friends and loved ones.

One day, Sarah received a call from Emily. She could tell from the tone of her friend's voice that something was wrong. Emily was crying on the other end of the line, and Sarah could feel her own heart breaking.

"What's wrong, Emily? Please tell me," Sarah said, trying to soothe her friend.

"It's my mom," Emily choked out between sobs. "She's been diagnosed with cancer."

Sarah's heart sank. She knew how much Emily loved her mother and how close they were. She felt helpless and didn't know what to say or do to make things better.

"I'm so sorry, Emily. Is there anything I can do to help?" Sarah asked, hoping to provide some comfort.

Emily took a deep breath. "I don't know, Sarah. I just feel so lost and alone right now. I don't know how to deal with this," she said.

Sarah knew that Emily needed her now more than ever. She promised to be there for her friend, to listen and support her in any way she could. She made plans to visit Emily the next day, and to bring some food and comfort to her and her mother.

The next day, Sarah arrived at Emily's house with a basket of fresh fruits and vegetables, as well as some homemade soup and bread. She hugged Emily tightly, feeling her friend's pain and sorrow.

As they sat together in the living room, Sarah listened as Emily shared her fears and anxieties about her mother's illness. She felt grateful to be able to provide some comfort to her friend, even if it was just a listening ear.

Over the next few weeks, Sarah spent more time with Emily and her mother, helping with errands, cooking meals, and providing emotional support. She watched as Emily grew stronger and more resilient, even in the face of such a difficult situation.

Through it all, Sarah was reminded of the power of love and friendship. She knew that life was full of challenges and hardships, but as long as she had her loved ones by her side, she could overcome anything.

As the days turned into weeks, Sarah continued to be there for Emily and her mother. She visited them regularly, taking them to doctor's appointments and helping with household chores.

Sarah could see how much Emily was struggling to cope with her mother's illness, and she knew that she needed more than just a listening ear. She encouraged Emily to seek professional help and even offered to go with her to her therapy appointments.

Emily was hesitant at first, but she eventually agreed to try therapy. Sarah was proud of her friend for taking that step, and she continued to support her every step of the way.

As Emily started to heal and find ways to cope with her mother's illness, Sarah couldn't help but feel grateful for the bond they shared. She knew that their friendship was built on a foundation of love and trust, and she felt privileged to be able to be there for Emily during this difficult time.

One day, as they were sitting together in Emily's living room, Emily's mother spoke up. "Thank you both for everything you've done for me and for Emily. You've both been such a source of strength and comfort to us, and we couldn't have gone through this without you."

Sarah felt a lump form in her throat as she realized just how much of an impact she had made in their lives. She knew that it wasn't always easy to be there for others, especially during times of crisis, but she also knew that it was the right thing to do.

As they hugged each other tightly, Sarah knew that their bond would only grow stronger as they faced whatever the future held together. She felt grateful for the power of love and friendship, and she knew that as long as she had those things in her life, she could overcome anything.

Days turned into weeks, and weeks turned into months. Emily's mother's condition continued to deteriorate, but Sarah was there every step of the way, supporting Emily and helping her through the tough times.

One day, as they were sitting together on the porch, Emily turned to Sarah with a serious look on her face. "Sarah, I need to talk to you about something."

Sarah could sense that this was important, and she gave Emily her full attention.

"I know that I've been leaning on you a lot lately, and I appreciate everything you've done for me and my mom. But there's something else that's been weighing on me," Emily said, her voice trembling slightly.

"What is it?" Sarah asked, her heart starting to race.

"I don't want to burden you anymore, Sarah. I need to start taking care of things on my own. I need to find a way to move forward, even if it means doing it alone."

Sarah felt a pang of sadness at Emily's words, but she knew that her friend was right. It was time for Emily to take charge of her life and find her own way forward.

"I understand, Emily. But just know that I'll always be here for you if you need me. You're not alone," Sarah said, placing a comforting hand on Emily's shoulder.

Emily gave Sarah a small smile, her eyes brightening with gratitude. "Thank you, Sarah. You've been such an amazing friend to me. I don't know where I'd be without you."

As they hugged each other tightly, Sarah knew that their bond would never be broken. Even if Emily had to find her own way forward, Sarah would always be there, cheering her on from the sidelines.

Together, they watched as the sun set over the horizon, casting a warm glow over the world. And as they sat there, Sarah knew that whatever the future held, they would face it together, one day at a time.

CHAPTER 9

Several months had passed since Emily's mother had passed away. Emily had gone through a period of intense grief and mourning, but with Sarah's support, she was slowly starting to find a sense of peace.

One day, Sarah received a phone call from Emily. "Hey, Sarah. I was wondering if you're free tonight. I want to take you out for dinner. There's something I want to talk to you about."

Sarah could sense the hesitation in Emily's voice, and she knew that whatever she wanted to talk about was important. "Sure, Emily. I'd love to join you for dinner. Where do you want to meet?"

They agreed to meet at a cozy Italian restaurant in the heart of the city. As they sat down and ordered their food, Emily took a deep breath and looked at Sarah with a serious expression.

"Sarah, I've been doing a lot of thinking lately, and I've come to a decision," Emily said, her voice steady but full of emotion.

Sarah waited patiently, sensing that this was something big.

"I want to start a foundation in memory of my mom. I want to do something to honor her memory and help others who are going through what she went through."

Sarah felt a lump form in her throat as she listened to Emily's words. She knew that starting a foundation would be a huge undertaking, but she also knew that Emily had the drive and determination to make it happen.

"That's a wonderful idea, Emily. I think your mom would be proud," Sarah said, her voice filled with admiration.

Over the course of dinner, they talked about the foundation, bouncing ideas off of each other and discussing the logistics of getting it off the ground. By the time they left the restaurant, they had a rough plan in place and a renewed sense of purpose.

As they walked to the car, Emily turned to Sarah with a smile. "Thank you, Sarah. I couldn't have done this without you. You've been such an amazing friend to me, and I'm so grateful for your support."

Sarah hugged Emily tightly, feeling a surge of pride and joy. "You're the one who's amazing, Emily. I can't wait to see what we can accomplish together."

As they drove home, Sarah knew that the future was full of endless possibilities. With Emily by her side, anything was possible. And she knew that they would continue to make a difference in the world, one step at a time.

In the following days, Emily and Sarah started to put their plan into action. They spent countless hours researching and networking, reaching out to potential donors and supporters of their foundation. Emily poured her heart and soul into the project, and Sarah was there every step of the way, providing her with the guidance and support she needed.

As they worked on the foundation, Emily and Sarah's friendship grew stronger. They laughed and cried together, shared their fears and hopes, and encouraged each other through the ups and downs of the journey. They were a true team, and they knew that they could accomplish anything as long as they had each other.

Finally, after months of hard work and dedication, the foundation was ready to launch. Emily and Sarah hosted a fundraising event, inviting their friends and colleagues to join them in celebrating the foundation's mission and goals. The event was a huge success, and they were able to raise a substantial amount of money to support their cause.

As the night drew to a close, Emily and Sarah stood outside, looking up at the starry sky. "I can't believe we did it," Emily said, a sense of wonder in her voice. "We created something amazing, Sarah."

Sarah smiled, feeling a sense of pride and satisfaction wash over her. "We sure did, Emily. And we're just getting started."

As they hugged each other tightly, Sarah knew that their friendship would always be the foundation of everything they accomplished together. And she knew that, no matter what challenges they faced in the future, they would always be there for each other, supporting and encouraging each other every step of the way.

Over the next few months, Emily and Sarah continued to work hard to grow and expand their foundation. They received more donations and support and were able to launch several new initiatives and programs to help those in need.

As they sat together in Sarah's office, looking at the latest progress report, Emily felt a deep sense of gratitude for her friend. "Thank you, Sarah," she said softly, tears in her eyes. "I couldn't have done this without you."

Sarah smiled warmly, placing a hand on Emily's shoulder. "You don't have to thank me, Emily. We did this together. We're a team, remember?"

Emily nodded, feeling overwhelmed with emotion. "Yes, we're a team. And I'm so grateful to have you by my side."

Sarah squeezed Emily's shoulder gently. "And I'm grateful to have you as my friend, Emily. We make a great team, don't we?"

Emily smiled, feeling a deep sense of joy and fulfillment. "Yes, we do. And I can't wait to see what we'll accomplish next."

As they continued to work together, Emily and

Sarah knew that their friendship was the foundation of everything they accomplished. And they knew that, as long as they had each other, they could make a difference in the world and help those in need.

CHAPTER 10

Months had passed since the launch of the foundation, and Emily and Sarah had seen incredible progress in their mission. The programs and initiatives they had launched were helping people in their community in ways they had never thought possible. They were changing lives, and it was all thanks to the hard work and dedication of their team.

As they sat in Sarah's office one afternoon, Emily suddenly spoke up. "You know, Sarah, I've been thinking. Our foundation is doing amazing work here, but I can't help but wonder... what if we could expand our reach even further?"

Sarah looked at Emily, intrigued. "What do you mean, Emily?"

"I mean, what if we took our mission beyond this city and started a national or even global foundation? We could help so many more people, Sarah."

Sarah sat in silence for a moment, considering Emily's words. "That's a big idea, Emily. But... it's not impossible. With the right resources and support, we could make it happen."

A spark of excitement ignited within Emily. "Yes! That's exactly what I'm thinking. We could do so much more if we just took that leap."

Sarah smiled, feeling a sense of pride in her friend's ambition. "Alright, Emily. Let's do it. Let's start planning for a national foundation."

Over the next several months, Emily and Sarah worked tirelessly to make their dream a reality. They secured funding, recruited a new team of passionate and dedicated individuals, and created a comprehensive plan for the expansion of their foundation.

As they sat together in Sarah's office, looking over the final details of the plan, Emily couldn't help but feel a sense of awe at what they had accomplished. "I can't believe we're really doing this, Sarah. We're expanding our foundation on a national level."

Sarah smiled, feeling a sense of pride and excitement. "Yes, we are. And who knows? Maybe one day, we'll be able to take it even further."

Emily grinned, feeling a sense of endless possibility. "Who knows indeed, Sarah. The sky's the limit when we're together."

With their expanded foundation now up and

running, Emily and Sarah found themselves facing new challenges and opportunities. They were constantly on the move, traveling to different cities and countries to meet with potential partners, donors, and program participants. It was a whirlwind, but they loved every minute of it.

As they sat in their hotel room in Tokyo, Emily couldn't help but feel a sense of awe at the city's bustling energy. "Can you believe it, Sarah? We're in Tokyo, running a global foundation. It's like a dream come true."

Sarah smiled, nodding in agreement. "It really is amazing, Emily. And it's all thanks to your vision and hard work."

Emily blushed, feeling a sense of gratitude for her friend's support. "No, it's thanks to both of us, Sarah. We make a great team."

Sarah chuckled, feeling a sense of camaraderie with Emily. "Yes, we do. And speaking of which, we have a meeting with a potential partner in an hour. We should get ready."

Emily nodded, feeling a sense of excitement at the prospect of meeting a new partner who could help expand their foundation's impact even further. As they got ready for their meeting, she couldn't help but feel a sense of pride and excitement for what they had accomplished so far, and what they could accomplish in the future.

The meeting with the potential partner went well, and Emily and Sarah left feeling optimistic about the possibilities for collaboration. As they walked back to their hotel, Sarah turned to Emily with a mischievous glint in her eye. "Hey, Emily, have you noticed anything about our travels lately?"

Emily raised an eyebrow in confusion. "What do you mean?"

Sarah grinned. "We've been to so many places, met so many people, and done so many amazing things. But there's one thing missing."

Emily frowned, not sure where Sarah was going with this. "What's missing?"

Sarah's grin grew wider. "We haven't had any fun. Like, real, uninhibited, let-your-hair-down fun. We're always working, always professional. We need to change that."

Emily laughed, feeling a sense of relief at the idea of letting loose a little. "You're right, Sarah. We do need to have some fun. But how do we do that?"

Sarah's eyes sparkled with mischief. "I have an idea. Let's go out tonight, hit up some bars, maybe do some karaoke. What do you say?"

Emily hesitated for a moment, feeling a sense of nervousness at the idea of stepping out of her comfort zone. But then she looked at Sarah's eager face and felt a sense of excitement growing within her. "Okay, let's do it. Let's have some fun."

CHAPTER 11

That night, Emily and Sarah put on their best outfits and headed out into the vibrant city of Tokyo. They walked down the neon-lit streets, feeling the energy and excitement of the city pulsing around them. They went into a few bars, trying different drinks and snacks and chatting with locals and fellow travelers.

As the night went on, Sarah dragged Emily into a karaoke bar, insisting they sing a duet together. Emily felt her nerves rising, but she couldn't resist Sarah's enthusiasm. They browsed through the song list and finally settled on a classic ballad. As the music started, Emily felt a surge of adrenaline, and she began singing with all her heart. She was surprised at how much she enjoyed the experience, and even more surprised at how good Sarah's singing voice was.

After their song was over, they were approached by a group of locals who had been watching their performance. The locals invited them to join their group, and Emily and Sarah found themselves spending the rest of the night dancing, singing, and laughing with their new friends.

As they stumbled back to their hotel room in the early hours of the morning, Emily felt a sense of exhilaration and contentment. She realized that Sarah was right - they needed to let loose and have some fun every once in a while. It was a reminder that even when they were working to change the world, they still needed to make time for themselves.

The next day, as they headed to their next meeting, Emily felt a renewed sense of energy and passion for their work. She knew that the memories they had made the night before would stay with her for a long time, and that they would inspire her to keep pushing forward, no matter what challenges lay ahead.

Their next meeting was with a local community organization that focused on environmental issues. The organization was led by a passionate young woman named Yuka, who spoke with an unwavering determination about the impact of pollution and climate change on her community.

Emily and Sarah listened intently as Yuka shared her experiences, her voice cracking with emotion at times. They were both moved by Yuka's passion and the urgency of the issue. Emily realized that this was exactly the kind of grassroots movement they needed to support in order to create meaningful change.

After the meeting, Emily and Sarah sat down in a nearby park to discuss their next steps. They talked about the different ways they could support Yuka's organization and other similar groups, such as providing funding, resources, and connecting them with other organizations and experts in the field.

As they talked, Emily felt a sense of excitement building inside her. She realized that this was what she had been searching for - a way to make a real difference in the world. She had always believed that change was possible, but now she was beginning to see how it could actually happen.

Over the next few days, Emily and Sarah met with several other local organizations, each one more inspiring than the last. They listened to stories of triumph and hardship, of determination and resilience, and they realized that there was so much more they could do to support these movements.

As their trip came to a close, Emily felt a mix of emotions - excitement for the future, sadness at leaving this vibrant city and the amazing people they had met, and a renewed sense of purpose and passion for their work. She knew that they still had a long way to go, but she was more confident than ever that they could make a real difference in the world.

The flight back home was a quiet one, as Emily and Sarah both reflected on their experiences in Tokyo. Emily knew that she had a lot to process and think about, but she also knew that she was ready to take on whatever challenges lay ahead.

As they landed back in their home city, Emily felt a sense of excitement building inside her. She knew that they had a lot of work to do, but she was more determined than ever to make a difference.

Over the next few months, Emily and Sarah continued to work with the organizations they had met in Tokyo, providing funding and resources, and connecting them with other experts and organizations in the field. They also began to explore ways to bring these grassroots movements to a wider audience, using their platform and influence to raise awareness about the issues they were fighting for.

It was a long and sometimes difficult journey, but Emily knew that it was worth it. She had found her purpose, and she was more determined than ever to make a positive impact on the world. As she looked back on her trip to Tokyo, she realized that it had been a turning point in her life, and she felt grateful for the experience and the lessons it had taught her.

CHAPTER 12

Months had passed since Emily's trip to Tokyo, and she had thrown herself into her work with renewed passion and purpose. She had become a prominent advocate for social and environmental causes, and her efforts had not gone unnoticed. She had been invited to speak at several events and had even been interviewed by a few major news outlets.

One day, Emily received an unexpected invitation to attend a gala event hosted by a prominent environmental organization. She was surprised and honored to receive the invitation and immediately accepted.

The night of the event, Emily arrived at the venue, a grand ballroom in a luxurious hotel. She was awestruck by the elegant décor, the fancy attire of the guests, and the air of excitement that permeated the room. She made her way to the reception area, where she was greeted by the organizers and introduced to several other attendees.

As she made her way through the crowd, Emily's eyes landed on a familiar face. It was Aidan, her ex-boyfriend, who she hadn't seen since the day they had broken up.

Emily's first instinct was to turn and leave, but before she could, Aidan spotted her and began to make his way over. Emily braced herself for the awkward conversation that was about to ensue.

"Emily, it's been a long time," Aidan said, his voice tinged with surprise.

"Yes, it has," Emily replied, trying to keep her tone neutral.

Aidan shifted awkwardly, clearly unsure of what to say next. "I heard about your work. It's really impressive," he said finally.

"Thank you," Emily said, not sure how to respond.

They stood in silence for a moment, until Aidan spoke up again. "Look, Emily, I know I messed things up between us. I was selfish, and I didn't treat you the way you deserved to be treated. But I want you to know that I've been doing a lot of soul-searching, and I've realized that I still have feelings for you. I know it might be too late, but I wanted to tell you how I feel."

Emily was taken aback by Aidan's words. She had never expected to hear him say anything like that, and she wasn't sure how to respond. She looked into his eyes, searching for any hint of insincerity, but all she saw was genuine remorse and regret.

"Aidan, I appreciate your honesty, but I'm not sure how I feel about this," Emily said finally.

"I understand," Aidan said, his expression falling. "I just wanted you to know how I felt. I won't bother you anymore."

With that, Aidan turned and walked away, leaving Emily standing alone in the crowded ballroom. She felt a wave of conflicting emotions wash over her. Part of her was tempted to give Aidan another chance, but another part of her knew that it was too risky to open herself up to that kind of hurt again.

As the night wore on, Emily did her best to put the encounter with Aidan out of her mind and focus on the event at hand. She listened to the speeches, mingled with the guests, and even bid on a few items in the silent auction.

But as the night drew to a close, Emily couldn't shake the feeling that something had shifted inside her. She realized that she had spent so much time focused on her work and her goals that she had forgotten about the other parts of her life that were important too, like her relationships with friends and family, and even her own happiness.

As she left the ballroom and made her way home, Emily made a decision. She was going to start living her life in a more balanced way, making time for both her work and the other important.

As the night progressed, the air grew colder, and the stars shone brighter. Elizabeth and Jack continued to sit by the bonfire, enjoying each other's company. They talked about their past, their hopes for the future, and everything in between. Elizabeth felt like she could talk to Jack about anything, and he seemed to feel the same way.

As they talked, Elizabeth couldn't help but notice the way the firelight danced on Jack's face, highlighting his strong jawline and rugged features. She found herself drawn to him in a way she had never experienced before.

As the night wore on, Jack stood up and offered Elizabeth his hand. "Let's go for a walk," he said with a smile.

Elizabeth took his hand and they walked away from

the bonfire, hand in hand. They strolled through the woods, the moonlight filtering through the trees, casting a soft glow on everything around them.

As they walked, Jack stopped suddenly and turned to face Elizabeth. "Elizabeth, I know we've only known each other a short time, but I feel like I've known you forever," he said, his voice low and serious.

Elizabeth felt her heart skip a beat. She had a feeling she knew where this was going.

"I know we come from different worlds, and our lives are very different, but I can't help how I feel," Jack continued. "I think about you all the time, and I want to be with you."

Elizabeth's heart was pounding in her chest. She had never felt this way before, and she wasn't sure what to do. She knew she was attracted to Jack, but was she ready for a relationship? Especially one that would be so different from anything she had ever experienced before.

As she stood there, trying to sort out her feelings, Jack leaned in and kissed her gently on the lips. It was a soft, sweet kiss that sent shivers down

Elizabeth's spine.

"I understand if you need time to think about this," Jack said, pulling back from the kiss. "But I just had to tell you how I feel."

Elizabeth looked up at Jack, her heart full of conflicting emotions. She knew she needed to think about this, but right now, all she wanted was to be close to him. Without a word, she leaned in and kissed him again, harder this time, letting her feelings take over.

As they broke the kiss, Elizabeth pulled away slightly, looking up at Jack. "I don't need any more time to think," she said, a small smile playing at the corners of her lips. "I want to be with you too."

Jack's face broke into a wide grin as he pulled Elizabeth into a tight embrace. They stood there in the moonlight, wrapped in each other's arms, feeling more alive than they had ever felt before.

From that moment on, they were inseparable. They spent every moment they could together, exploring the town, hiking through the woods, and simply enjoying each other's company.

As their relationship deepened, Elizabeth found herself opening up to Jack in ways she had never done with anyone else. She shared her fears and her dreams, and he listened and supported her every step of the way.

Together, they faced the challenges that life threw their way, never losing faith in each other or the love that bound them together.

As the days turned into weeks, and the weeks turned into months, Elizabeth knew that she had found the one she had been searching for. With Jack by her side, she felt like anything was possible.

And so, as they stood together under the stars, Elizabeth knew that she was ready for whatever the future held, as long as she had Jack by her side.

CHAPTER 13

Months passed, and Elizabeth and Jack's love only grew stronger. They had become an inseparable duo, always finding time for each other no matter how busy their schedules were. They spent their weekends exploring new places and trying new things, and their evenings curled up on the couch watching movies.

But despite their happiness, Elizabeth couldn't shake the feeling that something was missing. She had always been an independent woman, focused on her career and her goals, but now she found herself yearning for something more. She wanted to build a life with Jack, to create a home and a family together.

One evening, as they were sitting on the couch, Elizabeth mustered up the courage to broach the subject.

"Jack, can we talk?" she asked, fidgeting with her hands nervously.

"Of course, love. What's on your mind?" he replied, sensing the seriousness in her tone.

"I've been thinking a lot lately, and I realized that I

want to start a family with you," she said, looking up at him with hopeful eyes.

Jack's face broke into a wide grin. "Are you serious?" he asked, barely able to contain his excitement.

Elizabeth nodded, feeling a weight lift off her shoulders. "I know it's a big decision, but I want to build a life with you, Jack. I want to start a family and create a home together."

Jack leaned in and kissed her forehead. "I want that too, Elizabeth. More than anything."

And with that, they made the decision to start trying for a baby. They knew it wouldn't be easy, but they were willing to face whatever challenges came their way.

Weeks turned into months, and as they waited for good news, Elizabeth began to grow impatient. She couldn't help but feel like there was something wrong, that they would never be able to conceive.

But then, one morning, as she took a pregnancy test, everything changed. The positive result filled her with a mix of joy and disbelief, and she could hardly wait to share the news with Jack.

As soon as he got home from work, she ran to him, tears streaming down her face.

"Jack, we're going to have a baby!" she cried, holding out the positive test.

Jack's eyes widened in shock, and then a grin spread across his face. "We did it, Elizabeth. We're going to be parents."

For the rest of the night, they talked excitedly about their plans for the future. They would need to find a bigger apartment, and they would have to start thinking about baby names and nursery themes.

But none of that mattered in that moment. All that mattered was the love that they shared, and the family they were about to create.

As they arrived at the park, they saw the vast greenery with colorful flowers in full bloom. The birds were chirping, and the sound of the fountain added a calm atmosphere. They walked around the park and talked about their childhood, family, and shared their interests. Emma realized that her feelings for Ethan were growing stronger with each passing day. Ethan's company made her feel comfortable, and she enjoyed being around him.

As they approached a bench overlooking the lake, Emma stumbled on a rock and fell. Ethan quickly rushed to her side and helped her up. She felt embarrassed and apologized, but Ethan assured her it was fine and helped clean her scraped knee. Emma looked up into Ethan's eyes, and in that moment, she felt an intense connection between them. She couldn't help but feel drawn to him.

As they sat down, Ethan pulled out a small package from his pocket and handed it to Emma. "I know it's not much, but I saw this and thought of you," he said with a smile. Emma unwrapped the package and found a beautiful necklace with a small silver pendant. She was speechless, touched by his gesture.

"Thank you, Ethan. It's beautiful," she said, admiring the necklace.

"It's nothing compared to the beauty that's wearing it," he replied, making her blush.

They spent the rest of the day talking and enjoying each other's company, making Emma feel like she had known Ethan her whole life. She couldn't wait to see him again and find out where their relationship would go.

As the sun began to set, they decided it was time to head back. As they walked, Emma realized that she didn't want the day to end. She didn't want to say goodbye to Ethan just yet.

"Emma, I had a really great time with you today," Ethan said, breaking the silence.

"I did too," she replied, smiling.

"Would you like to do this again sometime?" he asked, nervously.

Emma's heart skipped a beat. "Yes, I would love that," she answered, trying to hide her excitement.

Ethan smiled, feeling relieved. "Great, how about we make plans for next weekend?"

Emma agreed, and they exchanged numbers. As they said their goodbyes, Emma felt a rush of emotions, and she knew that she had fallen for Ethan. She couldn't wait to see where this would lead.

As she walked back to her apartment, she

couldn't stop thinking about Ethan and the wonderful day they had together. She felt grateful for meeting him and for the unexpected turn her life had taken. She knew that things were still uncertain, but she was willing to take a chance and see where this would take her.

When she arrived at her apartment, she took out the necklace Ethan had given her and put it on. As she looked at herself in the mirror, she smiled, knowing that she had found something special with Ethan. She couldn't wait to see him again and find out what the future held for them.

CHAPTER 14

The week passed quickly, and Emma found herself eagerly anticipating her date with Ethan. She had been thinking about him constantly and couldn't wait to see him again.

As she got ready, she tried on several outfits before finally settling on a simple yet elegant dress. She styled her hair and applied a bit of makeup, feeling nervous but excited at the same time.

When Ethan arrived, Emma felt a jolt of electricity shoot through her body. He looked handsome as always, dressed in a suit and tie.

"Hi Emma, you look beautiful," he said, smiling warmly at her.

"Thank you, you look great too," she replied, feeling a bit flustered.

Ethan took her hand and led her to his car. As they drove, they talked and laughed, feeling comfortable and relaxed in each other's company.

Their destination was a cozy Italian restaurant with dim lighting and soft music playing in the background. They were seated at a table near the window, with a view of the city lights.

As they enjoyed their meal, they talked about their interests, dreams, and goals. Emma felt like she was getting to know Ethan on a deeper level, and she liked what she saw.

After dinner, they took a walk through the city, holding hands and enjoying the cool night breeze. They stopped at a park and sat on a bench, looking up at the stars.

"It's beautiful tonight," Emma said, breaking the silence.

"Yes, it is," Ethan agreed. "Emma, I wanted to tell you something. I've been thinking about you a lot this week, and I realize that I really like you. I know we've only been on a few dates, but I feel like there's something special between us."

Emma felt her heart race, and she knew exactly what Ethan was trying to say. "I feel the same way, Ethan," she replied, smiling.

Ethan took her hand and looked into her eyes. "Emma, will you be my girlfriend?"

Emma felt her heart swell with joy. She had been hoping that he would ask her that. "Yes, Ethan, I will be your girlfriend," she answered, feeling happy and grateful.

They kissed under the stars, feeling like they were on top of the world. Emma knew that this was just the beginning of their journey together, but she felt confident that they could face whatever challenges lay ahead as long as they had each other.

As they made their way towards the estate, Sophia felt her heart race with anticipation. She had always admired the grandeur of the estate from afar, but now that she was finally going to step inside, she felt a flutter of nervousness in her stomach.

As they approached the entrance, a butler opened the door and greeted them. He led them through the spacious foyer and into a sitting room where a fire was crackling in the fireplace. The room was furnished with plush sofas and armchairs, and Sophia couldn't help but admire the luxurious decor.

As they waited for Lord Harrington to arrive, Sophia's thoughts drifted back to the last time she had seen him. She remembered the warmth in his eyes and the gentle touch of his hand on her arm. She wondered if he still felt the same way about her.

Her thoughts were interrupted by the sound of footsteps in the hallway. The door opened, and Lord Harrington entered the room. Sophia felt her heart skip a beat at the sight of him. He looked as handsome as ever in his tailored suit, and his smile made her feel as though she was the only person in the room.

"Miss Smith, how lovely to see you again," he said, bowing slightly.

"Lord Harrington," Sophia replied, trying to keep her voice steady. "Thank you for inviting me."

"It's my pleasure," he said, motioning for her to take a seat. "I hope you don't mind, but I've asked my sister to join us. I thought you two might get along quite well."

Sophia nodded, feeling a pang of disappointment that they wouldn't be alone. But as Lady Harrington entered the room,

Sophia felt her spirit's lift. She was a kind, intelligent woman who immediately put Sophia at ease.

As they sat and chatted, Sophia couldn't help but feel grateful for this unexpected opportunity. She had never imagined that she would find herself in the company of such refined and cultured people. And as she stole glances at Lord Harrington, she couldn't help but wonder if this was just the beginning of something more.

Liam couldn't believe his luck. He was standing in front of the love of his life, Sarah, who he had been separated from for years. Seeing her again was a dream come true, but now he had to convince her to forgive him and give him another chance.

"Sarah, I know I made a mistake by leaving you, and I'm sorry," Liam said, his voice shaking with emotion. "But I never stopped loving you. Not for one moment. Please, can we start over? Can we try again?"

Sarah looked up at Liam, her eyes filled with tears. She had been hurt so deeply by his betrayal, but she couldn't deny the feelings that still lingered in her heart.

"I don't know, Liam," she said, her voice barely above a whisper. "It's been so long, and so much has happened."

"I know, but we can work through it," Liam replied, his heart racing with hope. "I'll do whatever it takes to make it up to you. I just need another chance."

Sarah took a deep breath, her heart torn between the pain of the past and the possibility of a future with Liam. After a long moment, she nodded.

"Okay," she said. "We can try. But it won't be easy."

Liam smiled, relief washing over him. "I know it won't be, but I'm willing to do anything for you."

As they walked away from the beach, hand in hand, Sarah couldn't help but wonder if they could truly make it work this time. Would their love be strong enough to overcome the challenges ahead? Only time would tell, but for now, Sarah was willing to take a chance on Liam and see where their second chance would lead them.

CHAPTER 15

Over the next few weeks, Liam and Sarah worked hard to rebuild their relationship. They spent every spare moment together, talking, laughing, and rediscovering the things they loved about each other. It wasn't easy, but they were both committed to making it work.

One evening, Liam surprised Sarah by taking her out to a fancy restaurant. As they sat across from each other, sipping wine and enjoying the elegant atmosphere, Liam reached across the table and took Sarah's hand.

"Sarah, I have something I want to ask you," Liam said, his eyes locked on hers. "Will you marry me?"

Sarah gasped, her heart pounding in her chest. She had never expected Liam to propose so soon, but she couldn't deny the joy she felt at the thought of spending the rest of her life with him.

"Yes, Liam," she said, tears streaming down her face. "I will marry you."

Liam beamed, relief flooding over him as he slipped the diamond ring onto Sarah's finger. He had never been so happy in his life.

Over the next few months, Liam and Sarah planned their wedding, pouring their hearts into every detail. They chose a beautiful outdoor venue, surrounded by trees and flowers, and invited all of their family and friends to share in their special day.

As Sarah walked down the aisle, her heart overflowing with love for Liam, she couldn't help but think about all they had been through to get to this moment. It hadn't been easy, but they had made it through the hard times, and now they were stronger than ever.

As they exchanged their vows, Liam and Sarah knew that they were meant to be together forever. And as they kissed for the first time as husband and wife, they both knew that their love was unbreakable, and that nothing could ever come between them again.

As the day wore on, the anticipation of the gala grew stronger. Max couldn't help but feel nervous about seeing Amelia again. It had been almost a year since they had last seen each other, and he wasn't sure what to expect.

He tried to focus on the preparations for the

event, but his mind kept wandering back to Amelia. Max couldn't shake the feeling that something was off between them. He had always felt a strong connection to her, but lately, things seemed strained.

As the sun began to set, Max got dressed for the gala. He chose a classic black tuxedo and polished his shoes until they gleamed. He wanted to look his best for Amelia, but he also wanted to make a good impression on the other guests.

When Max arrived at the gala, he was immediately struck by the grandeur of the event. The ballroom was filled with elegantly dressed guests, and the tables were adorned with beautiful floral arrangements. Max spotted Amelia across the room, and his heart skipped a beat..

He made his way over to her, and she greeted him with a warm smile. Max felt a rush of relief wash over him, and he couldn't help but smile back. They chatted for a few minutes, catching up on each other's lives, and Max felt the tension between them begin to ease.

As the night went on, Max and Amelia found themselves dancing together. Max couldn't believe how effortless it felt to be in her arms. He knew that he had missed her more than he had realized.

As they swayed to the music, Max felt a surge of emotion that he couldn't ignore. He leaned in close to Amelia and whispered in her ear, "I've missed you so much."

Amelia looked up at him, her eyes sparkling with emotion. "I've missed you too, Max," she said, her voice barely above a whisper.

Max felt a rush of joy flood his body, and he knew that he had to tell Amelia how he really felt. He took a deep breath and said, "Amelia, I know that we've been friends for a long time, but I can't ignore the way that I feel about you. I love you, Amelia."

Amelia's eyes widened in surprise, but she didn't pull away. Instead, she leaned in closer and whispered, "I love you too, Max."

Max couldn't believe what he was hearing. He had been so afraid to tell Amelia how he felt, but now that he had, he felt like he was on top of the world.

As the night drew to a close, Max and Amelia left the gala together, hand in hand. Max felt like he had finally found what he had been searching for all along.

As they walked out of the restaurant, the cool evening breeze swept across their faces, carrying with it the promise of a beautiful night. Mia linked her arm with Adam's, feeling the warmth of his skin against hers.

"You know, I've never felt like this before," Adam said, breaking the silence.

"What do you mean?" Mia asked, curious.

"I mean, I've never felt so... complete, I guess. I feel like I've been waiting my whole life for you, and now that I have you, I don't want to let go."

Mia's heart swelled with emotion. She felt the same way but had been too afraid to voice it. She stopped walking and turned to face him, her eyes locking onto his.

"Adam, I feel the same way. Being with you has opened up a part of me I never knew existed, and I don't want to imagine my life without you in it."

Adam leaned in, and their lips met in a gentle kiss, a promise of what was to come. They pulled away, smiling at each other, both knowing that their lives had changed forever.

As they continued walking, hand in hand, Mia couldn't help but feel grateful for taking a chance on love. She had never believed in soulmates or love at first sight, but Adam had changed that. He had come into her life and filled it with joy, happiness, and most importantly, love.

The night was still young, and they had a whole city to explore. Mia knew that with Adam by her side, anything was possible. Together, they would face whatever the future held, and she couldn't wait to see where their journey would take them.

CHAPTER 16

As soon as Stella entered the restaurant, she could feel a familiar tingle in her stomach. It was the same place where she had first met Jack, and the memories came flooding back. But she pushed them aside and walked towards the table where Jack was already waiting for her.

"Hi," he said, standing up to greet her.

"Hi," she replied, trying to keep her tone even.

He held out her chair, and she sat down, avoiding his gaze.

"How are you?" he asked, taking his seat across from her.

"I'm fine," she said, looking around the restaurant nervously.

"I'm sorry if I made you uncomfortable earlier," he said, his voice low.

"It's okay," she said, finally looking at him. "I just didn't expect to see you again so soon."

"I know," he said, his eyes softening. "But I wanted to talk to you. To apologize."

Stella nodded, not sure what to say. She had been

trying to avoid Jack since their last encounter, but now that they were face-to-face, she couldn't deny the feelings she still had for him.

"I'm sorry about the way things ended between us," he said, reaching across the table to take her hand.

Stella pulled away, feeling a surge of anger. "You didn't care about me then, so why do you care now?"

Jack sighed. "I was young and stupid. I didn't realize what I had until it was too late."

Stella shook her head. "That's not good enough, Jack. You hurt me. You can't just come back and expect me to forgive you."

"I know," he said, his eyes pleading. "But please, just hear me out. I want to make things right between us."

Stella hesitated, but something in Jack's tone made her want to listen. "Okay," she said, reluctantly.

Jack took a deep breath. "I've been thinking about you a lot lately. And I realize that I still love you, Stella. I never stopped."

Stella felt her heart skip a beat. "Jack, I..."

"I know I don't deserve a second chance," he said, cutting her off. "But I promise you, things will be different this time. I will make it up to you. I will show you how much I care."

Stella looked at him, unsure of what to say. She knew that she still loved Jack, but she couldn't forget the pain he had caused her. Was it worth taking a chance on him again?

As she looked into Jack's eyes, she saw the sincerity there, and she felt a flicker of hope. Maybe they could make it work this time. Maybe they could have the happy ending she had always dreamed of.

"Okay," she said, finally. "Let's try again."

As they walked hand in hand down the street, Emily couldn't help but feel that everything was finally falling into place. She had the job she loved, a beautiful home with the man of her dreams, and a future that was bright with possibilities.

But as they turned the corner, she saw a familiar face standing on the sidewalk. It was her ex-boyfriend, David, and he was staring right at her. Emily's heart sank, and she pulled her hand away from Jack's, suddenly feeling nervous and exposed.

David started walking towards them, and Emily could feel her heart racing with anxiety. She didn't know what he wanted, but she was terrified of what might happen if he confronted her in front of Jack.

"Emily," David said, his voice sounding strained. "We need to talk."

Jack stepped in front of Emily, his protective instincts kicking in. "I don't think she wants to talk to you," he said firmly.

David's eyes narrowed, and Emily could tell he was angry. "This doesn't concern you," he spat at Jack. "This is between me and Emily."

Emily felt a wave of panic wash over her. She didn't know what to do or say. All she wanted was for David to leave her alone so she could continue building a life with Jack. But she knew she couldn't just ignore him and hope he would go away.

Taking a deep breath, she stepped forward. "David," she said, her voice trembling slightly. "I don't think there's anything left to say between us. It's time for both of us to move on."

David's expression softened slightly, and Emily could see the hurt and confusion in his eyes. "I just want you to know that I still love you," he said quietly. "And I always will."

Emily felt a pang of guilt and sadness. She had cared for David once, and she didn't want to hurt him any more than she already had. But she knew that she couldn't go back to him, not after everything that had happened.

"I'm sorry," she said softly. "But it's over between us. I hope you can find someone who makes you happy."

David nodded, his eyes downcast. "I understand," he said, before turning and walking away.

As they watched him go, Emily felt a mix of relief and sadness. She knew it wouldn't be easy to forget about David and everything they had shared. But she also knew that she was with the man she loved now, and that was all that mattered.

As they drove through the winding roads of the countryside, Lily could feel her heart pounding in her chest. She couldn't believe that she was finally going to meet her birth mother after all these years. The emotions she had been bottling up for so long were finally starting to spill out, and she couldn't control the tears that began to stream down her face.

"Are you okay?" Alex asked, his voice full of concern.

Lily nodded, wiping away her tears with the back of her hand. "I'm just nervous," she admitted.

"I know," Alex said, reaching over to take her hand. "But you're doing the right thing. You need to know where you come from."

Lily squeezed his hand, grateful for his support. "I just hope she's not disappointed in me," she said quietly.

"She could never be disappointed in you," Alex said firmly. "You're an amazing person, Lily. And no matter what happens, I'll always be here for you."

Lily smiled through her tears, feeling her heart swell with love for Alex. She couldn't believe how lucky she was to have him in her life.

As they pulled up to the address her birth mother had given her, Lily felt her nerves kick into overdrive. She took a deep breath and stepped out of the car, Alex following closely behind her.

The front door opened before they even had a chance to knock, and Lily was face to face with the woman who had given her life. She was struck by how much they looked alike – the same curly hair, the same bright blue eyes.

"Hello," Lily said, her voice barely above a whisper.

"Hello, Lily," her birth mother said, tears streaming down her face. "I've been waiting for this moment for so long."

As they walked, the sun began to set, painting the sky in shades of pink and orange. Emma couldn't help but feel a sense of peace wash over her as she strolled through the quiet streets with James by her side.

They turned a corner and suddenly found themselves in front of a small park. James grinned and gestured towards it.

"Shall we?" he asked.

Emma nodded, smiling. They walked through the gates

and made their way to a bench, sitting downside by side. The park was deserted, the only sound coming from the birds chirping in the trees.

For a few moments, they sat in silence, enjoying each other's company and the tranquility of the park. Finally, James spoke up.

"I know this isn't the most romantic setting," he said, "but there's something I've been wanting to ask you."

Emma's heart skipped a beat. She turned to face him, her eyes locking onto his.

"What is it?" she asked, her voice barely above a whisper.

James took a deep breath before continuing.

"I know we've only been seeing each other for a short time," he said, "but I feel like I've known you forever. I can't imagine my life without you in it, Emma. I know this might be sudden, but I have to ask: will you be my girlfriend?"

Emma felt tears pricking at the corners of her eyes as she looked at James, her heart overflowing with emotion. She took his hand in hers and squeezed it tightly.

"Yes," she said, her voice full of certainty. "Yes, I will."

They sealed their new relationship with a gentle kiss,

the warmth of the sun still lingering on their skin. Emma felt like she was exactly where she was meant to be, and she couldn't wait to see where this new journey with James would take her.

As they walked back to the car, Emily noticed that Lucas seemed quieter than usual. She wondered if something was bothering him, but she didn't want to pry. They got in the car and drove back to Lucas's house in silence.

Once they arrived, Lucas turned off the engine and turned to Emily. "I need to talk to you about something," he said, looking serious. Emily's heart sank. She had a feeling she knew what was coming.

"What is it?" she asked, bracing herself.

"I'm leaving town," he said, and Emily felt her stomach drop. "My job is sending me to New York, and I have to leave in two weeks."

Emily's mind raced. She didn't know what to say. She had grown so used to having Lucas around, and the thought of him leaving was almost unbearable. "What about us?" she finally managed to ask.

"I don't know," Lucas said, looking pained. "I don't want to leave things between us up in the air, but I don't know if I can do long distance. It's not fair to either of us."

Emily felt tears prick at the corners of her eyes. She

didn't want to lose Lucas, but she also didn't want to hold him back. "I understand," she said, trying to keep her voice steady. "I just wish there was another way."

"I do too," Lucas said, reaching over to take her hand. "But sometimes life has a way of throwing us curveballs."

They sat in silence for a few moments, both lost in thought. Finally, Emily spoke up. "I want you to know that I care about you," she said, looking at Lucas. "And whatever happens, I want us to stay in touch."

Lucas smiled sadly. "I care about you too," he said. "And I promise I'll call and write and stay in touch as much as I can."

Emily nodded, feeling a sense of closure. It wasn't the ending she wanted, but it was an ending, nonetheless. She leaned over to give Lucas a hug, and he hugged her back tightly. As they pulled away, Emily couldn't help but feel a sense of sadness wash over her. She didn't know what the future held, but she knew that things would never be quite the same between her and Lucas again.

CHAPTER 17

After the wedding ceremony, the guests gathered in the ballroom for the reception. The newlyweds were seated at the head table, and the guests took their seats at the tables surrounding the dance floor.

The DJ played a soft melody, and the couple stood up to dance their first dance as husband and wife. They swayed to the music, lost in each other's arms. The guests watched with admiration, and some had tears in their eyes.

After their dance, the groom took the microphone to make a speech. "I want to thank everyone who came to celebrate this special day with us," he said, his voice filled with emotion. "I want to thank my beautiful wife for making me the happiest man alive. I promise to love you, cherish you, and support you in all that you do."

The bride stood up to make her speech, and the room fell silent. "I never believed in love at first sight until I met this amazing man," she said, her voice shaking with emotion. "You complete me in every way, and I'm so grateful to have you in my life. I promise to be your best friend, your partner, and your soulmate for the rest of our lives together."

The guests erupted in applause, and the couple shared a kiss, sealing their love in front of their loved ones. The rest of the evening was filled with dancing, laughter, and joy. The bride and groom were surrounded by love, and they knew that they were meant to be together forever.

As they sat there, watching the sun setting over the ocean, Elizabeth felt a sense of peace wash over her. She had never felt so content and happy in her life. She looked over at Jack and saw that he was watching her, a soft smile on his face.

"Thank you for bringing me here," she said, breaking the silence.

Jack reached over and took her hand. "I wanted to show you something beautiful," he said, squeezing her hand gently.

Elizabeth turned her hand over and laced her fingers with his. "It is beautiful," she said. "And so are you."

Jack chuckled. "You always know just what to say," he said, leaning in to kiss her.

As they kissed, Elizabeth felt her heart swell with love for this man. She knew that she was falling for him, and she didn't care. She wanted to be with him, to spend the rest of her life with him.

When they finally pulled away from each other, they both looked out at the ocean again. The sky was turning dark now, the stars starting to twinkle above them.

"Let's stay here for a while," Jack said. "I don't want to leave just yet."

Elizabeth smiled. "I'm in no rush," she said, leaning her head on his shoulder. "I could stay here forever."

As they reached the top of the stairs, Emily's heart was racing with anticipation. She could hear the sound of music and laughter coming from the ballroom, and she knew that this was going to be a night she would never forget.

As they entered the ballroom, Emily was struck by the sheer beauty of the room. The walls were adorned with gold leaf and crystal chandeliers hung from the ceiling, casting a warm and inviting glow over the room. The guests were all dressed in their finest attire, and the ladies' gowns sparkled in the light.

Emily and James made their way around the room, greeting their guests and making small talk. Emily felt a flutter in her stomach every time James smiled at her or brushed against her arm. She couldn't believe that this handsome and charming man was hers.

As they made their way to the dance floor, the orchestra began to play a waltz. James took Emily's hand and pulled her close, and they began to dance. Emily's heart swelled with joy as she gazed into James's eyes, feeling like they were the only two people in the world.

The dance ended too soon, and James led Emily to a table where they could rest and have some refreshments. As they sat down, James took Emily's hand in his and gazed into her eyes.

"Emily, I have something I need to tell you,"He said, his voice serious.

Emily's heart skipped a beat. She had a feeling she

knew what was coming.

"I love you, Emily. I know it may be soon, but I can't help how I feel. I want to spend the rest of my life with you. Will you marry me?"

Emily's eyes widened in shock and delight. She had been hoping and praying that James would propose, but she hadn't expected it to happen so soon.

"Yes, James. I will marry you," she said, her voice trembling with emotion.

James's face broke into a huge smile, and he leaned over to kiss Emily, sealing their engagement. The rest of the night passed in a blur of happiness and celebration, and Emily knew that her life would never be the same again.

CHAPTER 18

Jenna woke up to the sound of chirping birds outside her window. She stretched her arms and let out a deep sigh. It was a beautiful day, and she had no idea what to do with it. It was her day off, and she didn't have any plans.

She got out of bed and headed to the kitchen to make herself some coffee. As she waited for it to brew, she checked her phone and saw a message from Jack.

"Hey Jenna, are you free today? I want to take you out for a surprise."

Jenna felt her heart race with excitement. She quickly replied, "Yes, I'm free! What's the surprise?"

Jack replied with a wink emoji, "It wouldn't be a surprise if I told you now, would it?"

Jenna smiled to herself, feeling grateful that Jack was putting in so much effort into their relationship. She finished her coffee and got dressed for the day, wondering where Jack could be taking her.

When Jack arrived, he was holding a bouquet of flowers and had a huge grin on his face. "You look beautiful," he said, handing her the flowers.

Jenna blushed and thanked him. "So where are we going?" she asked, trying to contain her excitement.

Jack took her hand and led her to his car. "You'll see," he said, and they drove off.

As they drove, Jenna tried to guess where they were headed, but Jack remained tight-lipped. They drove for about an hour until they finally arrived at a small airport.

Jenna's eyes widened with surprise as Jack parked the car. "We're flying somewhere?" she asked, feeling a mix of excitement and nervousness.

Jack grinned at her. "Yep, we're going on a little adventure today."

Jenna's heart raced as they boarded the small plane. She couldn't believe Jack had gone through all this trouble for her. As they took off into the sky, Jenna looked out the window and felt a sense of freedom and excitement wash over her.

She turned to Jack, who was watching her with a

fond smile. "Thank you," she said, feeling a lump form in her throat.

Jack squeezed her hand. "Anything for you, Jenna."

As they flew off into the unknown, Jenna knew that she was falling even deeper in love with Jack. She couldn't wait to see where this adventure would take them.

As they walked back to the house, Rachel asked Ethan about his plans for the future. "Well," he began, "I've been working on a business plan for a while now. I want to start my own construction company. I've been saving up money for it and I think I'm almost ready to launch."

Rachel looked at him with admiration. "That's amazing, Ethan. I had no idea you were so entrepreneurial."

Ethan smiled. "Yeah, I've always been interested in starting my own business. And I think I have what it takes to make it work."

Rachel nodded. "I believe you do. And if you need any help or support, don't hesitate to ask."

"Thanks, Rachel," Ethan said, feeling grateful for her encouragement.

As they entered the house, they saw that the others were already sitting in the living room, chatting and laughing. Ethan introduced Rachel to his friends, and they all welcomed her warmly. They spent the rest of the evening playing board games and telling stories, and Rachel felt a sense of belonging she had never felt before. For the first time in her life, she felt like she had found a place where she belonged, with people who cared about her.

As the night wore on and everyone began to get sleepy, Ethan walked Rachel to the guest room. "Goodnight, Rachel," he said, giving her a gentle hug.

"Goodnight, Ethan," she replied, feeling a flutter in her chest.

As she closed the door and crawled into bed, she couldn't help but think about Ethan and the feelings he stirred in her. She knew that she was falling for him, and she didn't know what to do about it. All she knew was that she wanted to spend more time with him, to get to know him better, and to see where this could lead. She closed her eyes and drifted off to sleep, dreaming of a future where she and Ethan were together.

As the day turned into night, the guests slowly began to trickle out of the reception hall. The music had stopped, the food had been cleared away, and the happy couple had said their goodbyes. Emily and Alex were finally alone, sitting at a small table in the center of the room, holding hands.

"I can't believe it's over," Emily said, her voice filled with emotion.

"I know," Alex replied, squeezing her hand. "It all went by so fast."

Emily looked up at him, her eyes sparkling. "But it was perfect, wasn't it? Everything we ever dreamed of?"

"More than perfect," Alex said, leaning in to kiss her. "I never thought I could be this happy."

They sat in silence for a few moments, savoring the moment. Then Alex spoke up.

"You know, there's something I've been meaning to talk to you about."

Emily looked at him quizzically. "What is it?"

"Well, you know how we've been talking about starting a family?"

Emily's face lit up. "Yes, of course! I can't wait to be a mom."

Alex smiled. "I can't wait to be a dad, either. And I was thinking, now that the wedding's over, maybe we should start trying."

Emily's heart skipped a beat. "Really? You mean it?"

Alex nodded. "I do. I know we have a lot of adventures ahead of us, but I can't think of anything more exciting than starting a family with you."

Emily threw her arms around him, tears streaming down her face. "I love you so much," she whispered.

"I love you too," Alex replied, holding her close.

As they sat there, lost in their own world, they both knew that this was just the beginning of their happily ever after.

CHAPTER 19

As the sun began to rise over the horizon, Caroline lay awake in bed, staring at the ceiling. It was the day of the annual town fair, and she couldn't help but feel a sense of excitement and nervousness all at once.

She had been looking forward to the fair for weeks, ever since she found out that Michael would be working at the dunking booth. She had been thinking about him more and more lately, and the fair seemed like the perfect opportunity to spend some time with him.

Caroline got out of bed and began to get dressed, carefully selecting an outfit that she thought would impress Michael. She put on a white sundress and a pair of scrappy sandals, and then grabbed a small purse before heading out the door.

As she walked down the street towards the fairgrounds, Caroline could feel her heart racing with anticipation. She had never been the type to chase after a man, but something about Michael had captured her attention.

When she arrived at the fair, Caroline scanned the

crowd, searching for Michael's familiar face. She finally spotted him standing near the dunking booth, wearing a blue t-shirt and a pair of faded jeans. He looked up and saw her, and a smile spread across his face.

"Hey, Caroline!" he called out, waving her over.

Caroline felt her cheeks flush as she made her way towards him. "Hey, Michael. How's the dunking booth going?"

"It's going great," he replied. "Want to give it a try?"

Caroline hesitated for a moment, but then nodded. She handed Michael a few dollars and climbed up onto the platform. Michael handed her a ball and gave her a sly grin.

"Make sure you aim well," he said. "I wouldn't want to get too wet."

Caroline took a deep breath and threw the ball as hard as she could. It hit the target dead-on, and Michael tumbled into the water below with a loud splash.

Caroline laughed as he surfaced, shaking his head to get the water out of his hair. "Nice shot," he said, grinning at her.

They spent the rest of the day wandering around the fair, trying their luck at the games and sampling the various food stands. As the sun began to set, Michael suggested that they take a walk around the town square.

As they walked, Caroline felt a sense of contentment wash over her. She had never felt so comfortable around someone before, and she couldn't help but think that maybe Michael felt the same way.

As they reached the edge of town, Michael stopped and turned to face Caroline. "Caroline, there's something I need to tell you,"He said, his voice serious.

Caroline's heart skipped a beat. "What is it?"

Michael took a deep breath. "I know we've only known each other for a short time, but I feel like we have a connection that's hard to ignore. I really like you, Caroline, and I was wondering if maybe you feel the same way."

Caroline's heart leapt into her throat. She had been waiting for this moment for what felt like forever. "Michael, I like you too," she said, smiling up at him.

Without another word, Michael leaned in and kissed her, his arms wrapping around her tightly. Caroline felt a rush of warmth spread through her as she kissed him back, knowing that this was the start of something special.

As the day of the wedding drew near, both Emily and Jack were filled with a mix of excitement and nervousness. They had spent so much time planning and preparing for this day, and now it was finally happening.

Emily had chosen a beautiful white dress that accentuated her curves, and Jack had opted for a classic black suit with a white shirt and a red tie. They both looked stunning, and as they stood in front of the altar, they couldn't help but feel overwhelmed by the moment.

The ceremony was simple and heartfelt, with Emily and Jack exchanging their vows in front of their closest family and friends. There were tears of joy and laughter, and as they were pronounced husband and wife, the couple shared a loving kiss.

After the ceremony, the newlyweds and their guests made their way to a nearby reception hall for the party. There was music, dancing, and plenty of food and drinks to go around. Emily and Jack took to the dance floor for their first dance as husband and wife, and as they swayed to the music, they couldn't help but feel grateful for each other and the life they had built together.

As the night drew to a close, Emily and Jack said their goodbyes to their guests and headed off to their honeymoon. They were excited for the adventure ahead, but more than anything, they were looking forward to spending the rest of their lives together.

As the sun began to set, Emma felt a sense of contentment wash over her. She had spent the day exploring the town, and now she was sitting on the beach watching the waves roll in.

The events of the past few weeks felt like a distant memory now. She had come to this town to escape the pain and heartache of her past, and for the first time in a long time, she felt like she had made the right decision.

As she sat there, lost in thought, she heard a voice behind her. "Beautiful, isn't it?"

Emma turned around to see Adam standing there, a small smile on his face.

"Yes, it is," she said, smiling back at him.

Adam took a seat beside her, and they both sat in silence for a few moments, watching the waves crash against the shore.

"Emma, there's something I need to tell you," Adam finally said, breaking the silence.

Emma's heart skipped a beat. She had a feeling she knew what was coming, and she wasn't sure she was ready to hear it.

"I know we've only known each other for a short time, but I feel like I've known you my whole life," Adam said, taking her hand in his. "Emma, I love you."

Emma's eyes widened in surprise. She hadn't expected him to say those words so soon, but as she looked into his eyes, she knew they were true.

"I love you too, Adam," she said, feeling a sense of happiness she hadn't felt in a long time.

Adam leaned in and kissed her softly on the lips, and Emma felt her heart swell with love.

For the first time in a long time, she felt like she had found someone who truly cared for her, and she knew that she was ready to start a new chapter in her life.

CHAPTER 20

After their tearful reunion at the hospital, Olivia and Mark decided to take a short vacation to spend some quality time together. They rented a cozy cabin in the mountains, far away from the city's hustle and bustle.

As they settled into their new surroundings, Olivia couldn't help but feel grateful for this opportunity to escape the chaos of their lives and reconnect with Mark. She watched as he built a fire in the fireplace, marveling at how domestic and comforting the scene felt.

Over the next few days, they hiked through the woods, cooked meals together, and played board games by the fire. Olivia felt happier than she had in a long time, and she was glad to see Mark smiling again.

On their last night in the cabin, they sat outside and watched the stars twinkle in the sky. Olivia rested her head on Mark's shoulder, feeling content and peaceful.

"I'm so grateful for this time with you," she said, breaking the silence.

"Me too," he replied, his voice soft and warm. "I feel like we've been given a second chance, and I don't want to waste it."

Olivia nodded, feeling a surge of love for him. She knew that there would be challenges ahead, but for now, she was content to bask in the moment and soak up the love that surrounded her.

As they headed back to the city, Olivia felt hopeful for the first time in months. She knew that life would never be perfect, but she was determined to make the most of every moment and cherish the love she had found in Mark.

As soon as the words left his mouth, Sarah's heart started to race. She couldn't believe that James was asking her to marry him. It was something she had dreamed of for a long time, but now that it was actually happening, she was overwhelmed with emotions.

James watched her intently, his eyes full of hope and nervousness. He had always known that Sarah was the one for him, and he was thrilled at the prospect of spending the rest of his life with her.

For a few moments, Sarah couldn't speak. She just looked at James, her eyes glistening with unshed tears. Finally, she found her voice. "Yes," she whispered. "Yes, I will marry you, James."

Relief washed over James, and he let out a deep breath. "Thank God," he said, grinning from ear to ear. "I was so nervous; I wasn't sure what you were going to say."

Sarah laughed, feeling the tension in the air dissipate. "I think I was just in shock," she said, still staring at the diamond ring on her finger. "It's beautiful."

"I'm glad you like it," James said, taking her hand and bringing it to his lips. "I wanted to give you something that would always remind you of this moment."

Sarah leaned in and kissed him, feeling a sense of joy and contentment wash over her. She knew that there would be challenges ahead, but with James by her side, she felt like she could conquer anything.

As they walked hand in hand down the beach, Sarah couldn't help but think about the future. She knew that there would be highs and lows, but she was excited to face them all with James by her side.

As the team arrived back at their headquarters,

they couldn't help but feel a sense of accomplishment. They had successfully completed their mission, and the world was now a safer place. The group sat down for a debriefing, discussing their successes and areas for improvement.

As they finished up their debriefing, the team leader looked at each member and said, "I couldn't be prouder of each and every one of you. Your dedication, bravery, and quick thinking have saved countless lives. This is only the beginning. Our work is never done, and we must always be ready to defend our world against any threat that comes our way."

With those words, the team dispersed to rest, recharge, and prepare for whatever challenges awaited them in the future. They knew that they had made a difference, and they were ready to continue making a difference every day.